MONSTER
HUNTERS
confront the Goat Man

by Jan Fields
Illustrated by Scott Brundage

Calico

An Imprint of Magic Wagon
abdobooks.com

abdobooks.com

Published by Magic Wagon, a division of ABDO, PO Box 398166, Minneapolis, Minnesota 55439. Copyright © 2019 by Abdo Consulting Group, Inc. International copyrights reserved in all countries. No part of this book may be reproduced in any form without written permission from the publisher. Calico™ is a trademark and logo of Magic Wagon.

Printed in the United States of America, North Mankato, Minnesota.
102018
012019

Written by Jan Fields
Illustrated by Scott Brundage
Edited by Tamara L. Britton
Design Contributors: Candice Keimig & Laura Mitchell

Library of Congress Control Number: 2018947942

Publisher's Cataloging-in-Publication Data

Names: Fields, Jan, author. | Brundage, Scott, illustrator.
Title: Confront the goat man / by Jan Fields; illustrated by Scott Brundage.
Description: Minneapolis, Minnesota : Magic Wagon, 2019. | Series: Monster hunters set 3
Summary: The Monster Hunters head to Kentucky to investigate the Goat Man for their Discover Cryptids Internet show. They find that some of the locals dress as the Goat Man as a tourist attraction. But the team doesn't think that's the whole story!
Identifiers: ISBN 9781532133664 (lib. bdg.) | ISBN 9781532134265 (ebook) | ISBN 9781532134562 (Read-to-me ebook)
Subjects: LCSH: Monsters--Juvenile fiction. | Tourists--Juvenile fiction. | Internet videos--Juvenile fiction.
Classification: DDC [FIC]--dc23

TABLE of CONTENTS

chapter 1

THE FRESNO NIGHTCRAWLERS

"This is a terrible idea!"

"Ben liked it," Gabe Brown shouted up the hill to his best friend, Tyler. "And we're doing it."

Gabe and his friends worked for Gabe's brother to create an Internet show called *Discover Cryptids*. In each episode, they focused on a specific creature from myth or legend that may exist. When it came to the Fresno Nightcrawlers, Gabe was fairly sure those people were wrong. For one thing, the legend of the Fresno Nightcrawlers was really new compared to most of the other cryptids. Also, the whole tale depended on two blurry videos shot by security cameras at night.

Gabe hefted the small security camera they'd

bought only hours before and pointed it up the hill where a wide path sloped steeply down toward a small pond. He had better cameras in the van, but the team was trying to reproduce the original videos they had found on the Internet. In the videos, the creature looked like two legs and a lot of pale flapping fabric.

Gabe and Sean had a theory about how the strange videos were done and this shoot might just prove it. Gabe had to admit, his friends looked spooky as their white silky pants flapped in the breeze coming through the trees.

"Are you done messing with that camera yet?" Tyler yelled from the top of the hill.

"Almost."

"This is the goofiest thing you've ever made me do," Tyler complained, hiking the oversized pajama pants even higher and tucking them under his armpits. "Don't ever tell anyone I did this."

"No one will know it's you," Sean said mildly as he pulled on a black ski mask. "Just put your mask on."

"It's hot," Tyler complained, then he plucked at the sleeve of his black sweatshirt. "Everything about this getup is hot."

"You won't have to wear it long," Gabe said. He backed up as far as he dared. The ground near the edge of the pond was soft. Gabe didn't want to end up with his shoes covered in mud, so he held still and checked the view through the camera one more time.

In the shadowy darkness of the trees, the white pants stood out starkly and the black shirts blended into the night. Already it was hard to see Sean, and Tyler looked like a blond head floating over a pair of pants. "Put your mask on, and we'll get started," Gabe yelled. "Keep the ends of your sleeves over your hands and remember to let Sean start first. The creatures in the video didn't walk close together. Walk stiff legged. Think zombie walk."

"Yeah, yeah," Tyler said as he pulled the mask over his face. "Fine. When we're done, I want a milkshake."

"That can probably be arranged," Gabe said. Ben would be glad to have this piece of the episode done, especially if they could get it done in one take. "Let's go!"

Sean began shambling down the path, his joints sometimes loose and wobbly and sometimes stiff. Gabe was amazed at how much he looked like one of the Fresno Nightcrawlers. They might have landed on exactly how the video had been made.

Almost immediately after Sean began his awkward march downward, Tyler followed. Gabe frowned. Tyler had started too soon. The two pairs of pants almost blended together on the screen instead of looking like separate creatures. Now they would have to start over.

He opened his mouth to shout at his friends, but a teenaged couple walked out of the woods and onto the path directly in front of Sean and Tyler. The girl took one look at the ski masks and screamed, "Muggers!"

She spun and ran pelting down the hill.

The boyfriend stomped up to Sean and gave him a shove. "Stop scaring April!"

Sean staggered back a step or two with a squeak of surprise. The hem of the silky pajamas must have trailed under one foot because Sean tripped and fell, his arms pinwheeling. He landed directly on Tyler. The two hit the ground in a tangle of limbs and began to roll down the steep hill.

9

At the bottom of the hill, Gabe watched in horror, still shooting video. From where he stood, his friends now looked like a ball of flapping white wings. Gabe thought they might be inventing their own cryptid.

He didn't have long to think about it. April still ran from the supposed muggers. In fact, running down the steep hill seemed to have sent her almost out of control as she hurtled toward Gabe.

Gabe jumped backwards to avoid her smashing into him, but he'd forgotten how close he was to the edge of the pond. The soft ground crumbled and fell away the second he landed. With a bellow, Gabe plummeted into the cold water of the pond.

Fortunately, he managed to hold the camera in the air the whole time to keep it out of the water, but that made it harder to struggle from the muddy pond. He'd just gotten to his feet again when a screaming ball of flapping white wings tumbled the last feet down the hill and landed on top of him.

Tyler pulled the sopping wet ski mask from his head as he glared at Gabe. "I told you this was a terrible idea." For once, Gabe had to agree with him.

chapter 2

ON TO KENTUCKY

The *Discover Cryptids* van crept along neighborhood streets of Louisville, Kentucky. From the van's dashboard, Ben Brown's phone barked commands. Gabe thought all GPS systems sounded bossy, even the ones on smartphones.

He spotted a little kid throwing a ball for a scruffy dog. It looked like fun. "I can't imagine a goat monster living around here," Gabe said.

Tyler looked up from the comic book in his lap. "I can. Sometimes the nicest places are really creepy after dark. But the monster doesn't live in this neighborhood does it?"

"No it does not. The Pope Lick Monster, also called the Goat Man, supposedly lives under a railroad trestle," Sean pointed from behind them.

"That is five point four miles from here."

Gabe turned around in his seat to look at Sean. "I read that it's still an active railroad trestle." He caught a frown from his friend. Sean liked being the one who did all the research. "Trains pass over that trestle every day. The noise and vibration must be terrible."

"According to the legend," Sean interrupted. "The Goat Man likes the busy trestle. It lures people onto the trestle with hypnosis or by mimicking the voice of someone they know."

Tyler looked at him, wide-eyed. "Oh wow. Imagine hearing Ben yell for us and then, bam! We get smacked by a train."

Gabe winced. "I'd rather not imagine it. I like cryptids that don't consider it fun to hurt people."

"Well, none of us are going to get hit by any trains," Ben said from the front seat. "Because we aren't getting on the trestle. We'll do all our filming from a safe distance."

"That is the wisest choice," Sean agreed.

"Why Kentucky?" Tyler asked, closing his comic book and squirming in his seat belt. Tyler rarely sat still for very long. "Why would a goat monster want to hang out in Kentucky? Is this the goat capital of the United States?"

Everyone waited while Sean checked the Internet for the answer. "Though Kentucky isn't among the top goat milk producing states," he said, "it is among the top goat meat producing states."

"Goat meat?" Tyler yelped. "Ick. No wonder the Goat Man wants to push people off trestles."

"I doubt the two are related," Ben called back. "Goat men have been part of human folklore since the ancient Greeks."

"Besides," Sean said, "Louisville, Kentucky isn't widely known for its goats. It's really famous for race horses. This is where the Kentucky Derby is run."

Tyler perked up. "Can we go see that?"

"It's the wrong time of year," Sean answered. "But the derby is just one of the state's many attractions. Kentucky is the location of the world's longest cave, Mammoth Cave."

"Do goat men live in the cave?" Gabe asked.

Sean said, "The website doesn't mention goat men."

Sean shuddered. "That's okay. I don't like caves. Too creepy."

"Okay guys," Ben sang out as the van turned sharply before pulling up in front of a house. "We're here. Tyler, grab a voice recorder in case this guy doesn't want to be on video. Gabe, bring the small camera."

"And what does Sean carry?" Tyler asked.

"My brain," Sean said, tapping his head.

Gabe didn't even bother arguing. Sean usually managed to avoid doing much of the carrying jobs, though he hauled his laptop and tablet around most of the time. Gabe grabbed the small camera bag at his feet. Tyler dove under the last seat in the van and rooted through one of the smaller equipment boxes until he came up with the tiny voice recorder. As usual, Sean simply hopped out of the van door and stretched while he waited for them.

"I hope we didn't hold you up," Tyler grumbled as he walked by Sean.

"It's all right," Sean said cheerfully. "I'm used to it."

They followed Ben up the sidewalk to a two-story house with a wide front porch. When they reached the steps leading up the porch, Gabe jumped as Tyler clutched his arm and jerked him to a stop. "Look!" his friend squeaked.

"Where?" Gabe's gaze swept the area. He saw Ben tapping on the front door. He saw a porch swing and flowers hanging in baskets and sitting on the porch floor. The whole house looked like something out of a magazine. He certainly didn't see what had Tyler's eyes bulging. Tyler raised a shaky hand and pointed toward the last window that looked out on the porch near the front corner of the house. The window had lacy curtains, but Gabe could see that someone was peeking out at them.

"So?" he asked. "People tend to look out windows when someone shows up." He raised a hand to wave, but Tyler grabbed his wrist and jerked it back down.

For a moment, the fear on Tyler's face was replaced with annoyance. "Really? And how often do people have long white beards?"

"I don't know." Gabe shrugged. "Sometimes."

"And horns?"

Gabe jerked his attention back to the window and squinted. Tyler was right. Whoever was looking out at them with dark, empty eyes had a ragged white beard and horns!

chapter 3

WHERE'S THE GOAT MAN?

Before Gabe could yell for Sean and Ben to look at the window, the front door swung open, and a man about Ben's age looked out at them. He wore jeans with holes in the knees and a black T-shirt with a picture of the Goat Man printed on it. "You the *Discover Cryptids* guys?" he asked, frowning slightly as he saw Sean standing beside Ben. His frown deepened when he spotted Gabe and Tyler coming the rest of the way up the steps.

Ben ignored the expression and offered his hand. "We are. I'm Ben Brown, and this is my team." He gestured to each of them, offering their names. Ben never gave any explanation of why the rest of his team were all kids, and Gabe liked that. To his big brother, they were just the team.

Ben used to have a team of adults who helped make *Discover Cryptids*, but a television company had lured them all away to work on a different monster show. Gabe and his friends had offered to help. For a long time Gabe figured his brother would eventually hire more adults for the job, but Ben seemed happy with the way things were. And Gabe sure wasn't going to suggest they change anything.

"We came to hear about your Goat Man attraction," Ben said. "I assume you're Mr. Freed?"

The man scratched his ear. "Yeah, Chester Freed. You can call me Chester. The Pope Lick Monster Menace is strictly a fall attraction. We don't run in the summer. But I have the props and stuff and some photos, if you want to look at them."

"We'd like to ask you some questions too," Ben said. "You seem well versed in the legends. If we could get the interview on film?" Ben gestured to Gabe who held up the camera.

Before Chester could answer, Tyler pointed toward the corner of the porch. "Who's the Goat Man in the window?"

Everyone looked at the window. The face was gone. Chester frowned at Tyler. "Was that some kind of joke?"

"No," Tyler stammered. "I saw a Goat Man. He had horns and everything." He turned a panicky face toward Gabe. "You saw it too, right?"

"I thought I did," Gabe said.

"There's nobody in costume in here, and the props are kept in a closet," the man said. "I've been brainstorming some new bits for the attraction, but it's way too early to mess with costumes. Maybe you boys saw some shadows."

He smiled at Ben. "I reckon vivid imaginations kind of come with your show, right?"

"Not usually," Ben said, giving Gabe and Tyler a frown of his own. "Could we come in and start the interview?"

Chester shrugged. "Sure, come on."

Chester led them into the living room of the old house. The room was cluttered with worn furniture and glass curios cupboards. A tall thin man with a scraggly beard sat perched on one of the arms of the sofa.

"This is Jake," Chester said. "He works on the attraction with me. We've been coming up with ideas for next year."

"New Goat Man ideas?" Sean asked.

Jake snorted. "Not if I get my way. We need to ditch the Goat Man. Nobody cares about it anymore. Zombies are where the haunted trail scares are these days."

"We are not switching to zombies," Chester

said. His tone was weary as if he'd said those exact words over and over. "Goat Man is the perfect angle for our location. Plus, it's what makes us different."

"Different isn't always better," Jake insisted.

Ben cut into the argument. "So how many years have you been doing the Goat Man theme?"

The question pulled Chester's attention back to the interview. While Chester answered Ben's questions about the attraction, his friend just crossed his arms over his chest and rolled his eyes.

As the men talked, Tyler held up the small recorder and Gabe filmed. Sean had no specific job, so he peered into the curio cupboards, staring at each small figurine.

"Why do you have so many little figurines?" Sean asked when Ben began to wind down his questions.

Chester's cheeks pinked slightly. "They're not mine. They belong to my mom."

As if the word "mom" had been magic, a tiny old lady with a cloud of white curls came into the room, carrying a huge tea tray filled with glasses. She wore a T-shirt that matched the one Chester wore over lavender sweatpants and sneakers that lit up as she walked. "I knew I heard extra voices in here. I brought you boys a little snack!"

Chester's face reddened even more. "Thanks, Mom, but we don't need a snack."

"I don't know," Jack said. "I probably need a snack."

Chester's mother pointed at Jack. "You eat like locusts on a field, so be sure to leave some for the children." She beamed at the three boys. "I know how growing boys need food. You boys have some cookies. I made them this morning."

The boys glanced at Ben, and he nodded.

"We could take a short break since your mom went to all this trouble." Chester sighed deeply, but he didn't argue.

The boys gathered around the tray, grabbing icy glasses of lemonade and cookies. Gabe politely took one cookie, though he noticed Tyler had a handful, some of which he was shoving into his pockets. He tried to catch his friend's eye to shake his head, but Tyler wouldn't look at him.

"So you boys are here to talk about the Goat Man?" The woman's blue eyes sparkled with interest. "Chester's Halloween attraction is very popular because of the Goat Man, even if he won't let me be in it."

"Mom," Chester growled. "Now is not the time to go through that again."

Jake stood up, holding up his hands. "That's my cue to leave. I've heard this particular argument before." He leaned down to grab an overstuffed duffle on the floor near his feet.

"What's in there?" Chester asked. "I didn't see you come in with a bag."

Jake laughed. "I could have come in with my head in my hands and you'd not notice, not when you're in brainstorming mode."

"So what is that?"

"Laundry. This isn't my only stop today. I'm off to visit my own mom and do my laundry." Chester's mother scowled at him.

"That sounds about like you," she said. "You probably don't even have a present for the poor woman."

Jake's grin got even bigger. "Just seeing me is present enough." He sauntered out and Chester's mother poked her son in the chest.

"You'd best not be thinking that way about me," she said.

Chester held up his hands. "Never."

"And you ought to let me be in the haunt."

Chester groaned. "Mom."

His mother rolled her eyes. "Right. Because little old ladies can't be scary. I know. You ought to know, little old ladies can be terrifying."

"You're certainly scaring me," Chester said.

Gabe wondered if Chester ought to be a little more worried. He thought of his own mother. It was never a good thing when she got mad. *I'd rather face a cryptid anytime than an angry mom*, he thought.

chapter 4

A MYSTERY APPEARS

Finally, Chester's mother lost interest in the argument. Instead she turned and gestured toward the camera that hung around Gabe's neck. "So are you boys working on a school project?"

Sean answered even though she'd clearly been talking to Gabe. That wasn't a huge surprise. Sean loved answering questions. "No, ma'am. School's out for the summer. We're working on an Internet show, *Discover Cryptids*."

The woman frowned. "What is a cryptid?"

"A legendary creature," Sean said. "In this case, the Goat Man."

She nodded, making her white curls sway. "I've seen him, you know. When I was just a girl. Of course, that was before they put up the big fence around the trestle." Her face turned serious. "Not that I think the fence is a bad idea. It should be huge. That area is dangerous."

Chester sighed. "Mom worries."

"Of course I worry," she said. "People have been hurt. As least Chester's attraction pulls people's attention away from the trestle."

"Really?" Ben said. "I didn't know that."

Chester nodded. "We focus on the woods as the home of the Goat Man. Actually, I'm not sure that isn't true anyway. Even if the Goat Man sometimes visits the trestle, he couldn't live there. He'd be seen all the time. He has to live in the woods."

"That is logical thinking," Sean said.

"Thanks," said Chester.

Ben spoke quickly, clearly wanting to get the conversation back on track. "I'd like to ask a couple more questions about the attraction."

He gestured to Gabe to begin filming again, and turned to look at Chester. "How many visitors do you normally have each season?"

"Hundreds and more every year." He glanced toward his mom who was rearranging the cookies on the tray. "There are dozens of Halloween attractions around here, but I think we offer something special."

"Could be better," his mother muttered. "If he'd let me be in it."

Ben glanced at Chester's mom, but continued as if she hadn't spoken. "Okay, you've told us that your version of the Pope Lick Monster legend has the Goat Man living in the woods. Anything else unusual about your telling?"

"We play with the story of the train wreck that released a Goat Man into the wild. Basically the Goat Man origin stories run to one of two." He ticked them off his fingers. "The Goat Man is the result of a curse or the Goat Man escaped from a circus train after a wreck."

Sean spoke up then, his arms folded over his chest. "I've done considerable research and I can't find records of a circus train actually wrecking on the trestle."

"It's a story." Chester shrugged. "It doesn't have to be true."

Gabe could tell by his brother's expression that he especially liked that quote. "Well," Ben said. "We won't keep you much longer. You said you might be able to show us some of your props? That would be great for the episode."

"Sure, it's all back here."

Chester's mother frowned at them as they filed out to follow to a narrow shadowy hallway. "Be careful back there. It's a mess. Don't let anything fall on those children!"

"She seems to think we're toddlers," Tyler grumbled as they followed Chester down to the end of the hallway.

"I keep everything in these back rooms." Chester threw open one of the doors, and Gabe gasped as something big and hairy tumbled out, landing in Chester's arms and sending the man staggering backwards.

"Goat Man!" Tyler shrieked.

Gabe had to peel Tyler off the front of him as the other boy had nearly run him over in his hurry to get away from the hairy creature in Chester's arms.

"Not the Goat Man," Chester said, as he struggled to heft the beast back into the room. "This is our gorilla costume. I don't know why it was leaning on the door. We keep both of the full body costumes in here on mannequins since they don't exactly fold up. The gorilla's mannequin must have fallen over."

"Why do you need a gorilla at a Goat Man attraction?" Sean asked.

Chester grunted as he pushed at the heavy mannequin. "In our attraction, the Goat Man isn't the only scary thing that escapes from the train wreck. Gorillas are scary." Then he grinned over his shoulder at the boys. "And the gorilla costume was on sale."

"If the Goat Man costume is as scary as that gorilla, it must be great," Ben said as he stepped up to help Chester drag the gorilla back into his spot inside the crowded room. Much of the rest of the space was taken up with large plastic bins

34

and cardboard boxes. Big wooden signs leaned against one wall.

Once they had the creature propped back up, Chester put his hands on his hips and looked around, scowling. "I thought I left the Goat Man in here with the gorilla. It must be in the other store room. Come on."

They walked across the shadowy hall, and Chester pulled on the heavy wooden door, but it wouldn't budge. "These old doors swell and stick." He hauled hard on it, and it flew open with a rush of dusty air that made the man sneeze. The boys tried to peek around him, looking for another hulking figure, but the room seemed full of nothing but boxes.

"Where's the Goat Man costume?" Gabe asked. He saw something half leaning out of a closet at the far side of the room. It looked like a pale man with no face. "Is that the mannequin?"

Chester rubbed his nose with the back of

his hand as he stepped over boxes and slipped between piles. He pulled open the closet door, extending his other hand to keep the pale figure from falling out. "Yeah, this is the Goat Man's mannequin. He should be right here. I don't know where he is."

"I told you I saw a Goat Man looking out a window," Tyler insisted. "Maybe someone is wearing the outfit right now."

Maybe Jake, Gabe thought, though he wasn't sure how Chester would feel about him blaming his friend so he kept quiet.

chapter 5

The Trestle

Ben leaned against one wall of the small room. "It's interesting that the Goat Man suit vanished just as we came to do our show."

Chester wiped a smudge off the empty mannequin. "There's no telling how long it's been missing. Someone could have taken the suit any time after last fall when we packed them away. I haven't come in here since then."

Sean ran a finger over one of the piles of boxes. "Someone has. These boxes are coated with dust, but the floor is really clean. No tracks, no sign of drag marks."

"Maybe Chester's mom cleaned the floor," Gabe suggested. She seemed like someone who wouldn't want a lot of dust in her house.

"No, Mom won't clean up in here until I let her be in the attraction," Chester said. "She's mad at me, but I can't put her in the show. Can you imagine anyone being scared of her? Especially when she starts lecturing people on being careful or not tripping in the dark."

"Maybe she couldn't stand the mess," Gabe said. "So she cleaned in secret."

"If Mom cleaned this place, she wouldn't have left dust on all the boxes." He ran his fingers through his hair, making it stand up wildly. "Look, I'm sorry I don't have the Goat Man to show you. I've got some photos and some video of the Goat Man in action, if that will help."

"Sure, we'd like to see those," Ben said. "But I do wonder where your Goat Man suit went. That's a pretty specific thing for someone to come in and steal."

"I'm sure it's not stolen," Chester said. "Sometimes some of my buddies come and borrow stuff if they're going to costume parties or doing prank videos. I mean, usually they ask, but it could be something like that. I'll ask around. I'm sure the suit will turn up. Why would someone break into my house just to steal a Goat Man outfit?"

Gabe thought that was a very good question. He also thought Jake would be a good person to ask that very question. He looked at Ben, thinking his brother might ask it, but Ben just crossed his arms over his chest and watched Chester poke around.

"Oh Chester, don't let the children in there." They turned to see Chester's mom peering into the storage room. "They could get hurt on some of that junk you have in there." She pointed at the wall near Sean. "Look at that. It's a scythe, right next to that little boy."

Sean puffed up, clearly offended, but before he could say anything, Ben spoke up. "Thank you for your concern, Mrs. Freed, but my team is very safety conscious. You don't have to worry."

The woman sniffed. "Of course I need to worry. I'm a mother. That's what we do."

Gabe thought about his own mom. He was grateful she didn't fuss. If she was like Mrs. Freed, she would never have let Gabe go with his brother to film the show. "We'll be really careful," he told her.

"Just be sure you do," she said, pointing at him. "Just be sure you do."

Gabe stepped back from the cranky woman and tried changing the subject by turning back to Chester again. "If one of your friends borrowed the suit, maybe they returned it but not to the right spot. That door was really stuck. Maybe your friend couldn't get it open. Could the Goat Man be stuffed in a closet somewhere?"

"Don't be silly," Chester's mom said, her tone almost angry. "If there were a dirty, hairy costume in any of these rooms, I'd know it."

"Yes, ma'am," Gabe said. "But maybe someone put it in recently? Tyler and I thought we saw something in the room with the windows looking out on the porch."

The tiny woman put her hands on her hips, and Gabe suddenly worried that she was going to throw them all out. He wasn't sure how he'd made her so angry, but he figured Ben wouldn't like that he'd annoyed the woman. Luckily Chester saved the day. "It can't hurt to look, Mom."

"Well, I don't have time for such silly behavior," she said with a sniff. "I'll go clean up the snack things." She spun on her heel and stomped away.

"Sorry about my mom." Chester hunched his shoulders and shoved his hands in his pockets. "I'll show you the rooms on this floor. I can't imagine any of my friends hauling the suit upstairs when it would be easier to put it back in the store rooms or leave it on the porch." Then he grinned. "Though that would have surprised the neighbors."

Ben chuckled. "You're probably right about that."

The team joined Chester on a short search of the first floor. They made sure to check every closet and shadowy spot, but the Goat Man suit didn't turn up. Finally they ended up in the room with the window that looked out on the end of the porch.

"This is my mom's office," Chester said. "She does the bookkeeping for our attraction and a bunch of other businesses around here."

Ben nodded toward a door. "Is that a closet?"

Chester shook his head. "It's the downstairs bathroom." He walked over and tried the door but it wouldn't open.

"I'm in here," his mother's high voice called

42

through the door. "Go away and leave me in peace."

"Sorry, Mom," Chester said. He turned to look at the others. "We don't need to look in there anyway. I think if the Goat Man was in that bathroom, Mom would notice."

"Well, I did see it through that window," Tyler insisted, pointing across the room. "When we first got here. I'm sure of it."

"Honestly," Gabe said, not wanting Tyler to feel abandoned. "I really thought I saw it too." Once again, he thought about mentioning Jake's bulging bag, but he'd already made Chester's mom mad, he hated to annoy Chester too.

"It's not here now," Chester said. "I don't know what to say."

"I do," Ben said, then he held out his hand to Chester. "Thank you for giving us your time. And I hope you find your suit. If you could e-mail us the photos and videos you mentioned?"

"Sure, no problem," Chester answered, shaking Ben's hand. "Thanks for coming by. I'll watch for the episode."

"Sounds good." Ben herded the boys outside, though Tyler was clearly sulking a little.

He stayed quiet as they drove out to a stretch of overgrown land surrounded by a chain-link fence. Gabe bent to look up through the windshield. "Is that the Goat Man's trestle?" He couldn't believe how high the trestle was. "I agree with Chester. If I was the Goat Man, I'd rather keep my feet on the ground."

"That's got to be as high as a skyscraper," Tyler said.

"At the highest spot, the drop from the trestle to the ground inside that fenced area is more than 80 feet," Sean said. "That would be about the same as an eight story building. Not exactly a skyscraper."

"Bet it feels like one if you fall off," Tyler grumbled.

"You're probably right," Ben said. "That's why none of us is going to fall off it. We're staying safe on this episode."

Gabe felt the oddest shiver run up his spine. Why did that sound like famous last words?

chapter 6

ONE SCARY STORY

After they piled out of the van, they walked across dusty ground dotted with clumps of crabgrass and weeds until they reached the tall chain-link fence. Ben walked along the fence, looking through the chain-link at the brush beyond.

"How are we going to get in there?" Tyler tilted his head back to see the top of the fence. "That fence is high."

"We are not going in there," Ben answered, his voice firm. "We're going to shoot a quick scene near the fence. I'd like to find a spot where the trestle will show in the background."

"Why show the trestle?" Gabe asked.

"Because I want to make it very clear for the

viewers that no one should go in there and no one should climb that thing. Mrs. Freed was definitely right about that." He pointed at Sean. "Do you have the info I asked for?"

Gabe looked at Ben in surprise. He hadn't heard his brother ask Sean for any information. Sean bobbed his head, not speaking, and Ben said, "Good, let's go then. Gabe, run back to the van and grab the camera. Tyler, get the boom mic."

"And Sean," Tyler said loudly as he trotted back toward the van. "Don't forget your brain."

"Already got it," Sean called back. "I'll just wait here."

The team soon set up near the fence. Ben stood with his back to the chain link and the overgrown land on the other side. Though Gabe shot upwards toward Ben's face he could only catch some of the trestle support rising into the sky in the background. The trestle was simply too high to appear in the same shot as Ben's face.

Ben turned a serious face toward the camera. "Behind me is the railroad trestle where the Goat Man is said to lure people to their deaths. In real life, it's the legend itself that has proven to be the strongest lure." He then talked about the number of injuries and deaths caused by people sneaking onto the land and either falling from the trestle or being hit by trains.

Gabe kept the camera on Ben but his gaze drifted toward the trestle and shuddered. It was so high! Then as he turned his attention back to his brother, he gasped. Something moved in the brush behind Ben. Something was out there!

"Ben!" Gabe said, his voice high and thin. He pointed toward the brush behind his brother. Ben spun around, peering through the chain-link fence at the moving brush.

"Hello!" Ben called. "Is someone there?"

Tyler took a step toward Gabe, but he never

lowered the mic he carried on the long boom. Gabe figured if Tyler could be brave, so could he, so he took a step closer to the fence, aiming the camera to catch the moving brush.

A man in a dark shirt and matching pants stepped out of the brush. He had a neatly-trimmed white moustache and wore a badge pinned to his shirt. Gabe let out a whoosh of breath then he realized he was seeing a police officer.

"Hello," the stranger said. "You boys weren't thinking of climbing that fence were you?"

"No, sir," Ben said. "We're filming a show about the Goat Man myth, but this is as close as we planned to get to the trestle."

The police officer's expression darkened. "I wish you wouldn't bring any more attention to this legend. People get hurt that way."

"Don't worry. We're making it clear that the trestle is very dangerous," Ben said. "But if you don't mind, sir, why are you in there?"

"I walk this piece of land every day," the man said. "Just to make sure no one is getting themselves in trouble over here."

"You ever seen the Goat Man?" Tyler asked.

The police officer looked at Tyler silently for a long, silent moment. "I can't say for sure," he said finally. "I've seen some strange things in my life. Some of them were on this land."

"Do you mind telling us about it?" Ben asked.

The man glanced at the watch on his wrist. "It's time for me to go on break. How about you boys join me for lunch? I'll tell you a story. It's up to you what you make of it."

Ben's face stretched into a big smile. "That sounds fantastic."

They followed the police car to a small diner squeezed between a hardware store and a laundromat. Since it was early for lunch, the diner was mostly empty, giving them their choice of seats among the worn booths and scattering of round tables and chairs. The boys and Ben squeezed into one side of a large booth while the police officer sat on the other.

The police officer introduced himself then as Burt Silver, and promised to share his story as soon as they had some food. "Good food helps something like this go down," he said.

Once they had burgers and milkshakes, the police officer took a big bite of his burger. He chewed silently while the boys fought the urge to squirm with impatience. Finally, he spoke.

"I used to make my sweep of that property at night," the officer said. "You're more likely to catch pranksters then. It was a dark night, cloudy and without a moon. My flashlight had seen better days and better batteries, so I stomped around in the brush trying not to trip and fall." He turned a smile toward the boys. "I've fallen down a time or two."

"Me too," Tyler said.

"That night, I managed to keep my feet under me, but I was jumpy as a cat. I'm not afraid of the dark, mind you. I'm too old for that. But on the land under that trestle it's hard to relax."

"I don't think I could relax in a dark woods anywhere," Tyler said.

"There could be an electromagnetic field in the area," Sean suggested. "I saw some power lines not far from there. Some people report feeling edgy when close to charged air."

"I don't know about that," Officer Silver said. "But I know I felt edgy that night. So I walked as softly as I could. The trestle loomed above me, total black against the charcoal gray of the sky. I felt a rumble in the ground, and I knew a train was coming, though I'd not known one was expected. I stood looking up, waiting for the train. That's when it happened."

"What?" Tyler whispered.

"The footsteps. I heard footsteps clearly ringing against the rocks at the bottom of the trestle. I thought someone had climbed over the gate, so I picked up my pace and shouted. 'Stop! Police!'"

Gabe held his breath. He could almost see the scene in his head. They'd certainly run through more than their share of dark woods. "Did you catch him?" he asked.

"I thought I would," Officer Silver said. "I wasn't far away. I reached the rocks but no one was there so I flashed my light around. It was a terrible flashlight, as I said. It barely pushed at the darkness, but I didn't see anyone. I didn't hear anyone."

"Maybe it was your imagination," Sean suggested.

"I thought that," the officer agreed. "Then I heard something above me. I swung the flashlight up. Something clung to one of the supports for the trestle at least fifteen feet above my head. My light wouldn't quite reach it, but it was big. I yelled for the person to come down."

"Did he?" Tyler whispered.

"For sure," the officer agreed. "He jumped right at me!"

chapter 7

INTO THE WOODS

Officer Silver brought his hand down on the table with a loud smack. Gabe, Tyler, and Sean jumped in their seats and even Ben twitched a little.

"The Goat Man landed on you?" Tyler whispered.

"Nearly," the officer said, dropping his voice to a hoarse whisper. "I didn't see whoever it was, and he didn't land on me. But he did manage to knock the flashlight out of my hand. And when it hit the ground, it went out.

I was standing there in the pitch dark trying to grab whoever had just hit the ground beside me. I figured the guy had to be hurt. It was a long fall."

Gabe leaned forward on the table. "Did you find him?"

"Nope. But I heard him crashing through the bushes. I ran after him as fast as I could manage in the dark. I couldn't keep up, not without risking smacking face first into a tree. Whoever jumped off that trestle must have had eyes like a cat. He never slowed down."

"So you never saw him again?" Sean asked.

"I didn't say that either. When I broke out of the brush, I did see him one last time. He was against the chain-link fence and the light from the road shone through for just a second. I could only see the person in outline. But whoever stood there was tall, really tall and his head looked funny."

"Like he had horns?" Tyler asked.

"I don't know. I couldn't see him that well. It could have been some weird kind of hat. Maybe even a night vision rig. Or a costume. People have weird ideas when it comes to pranks. But I can tell you this, whoever it was didn't climb the fence. He doubled back into the brush and I never saw him again after that. I've never seen anyone in there since, but I keep patrolling, just to keep people safe." Then the officer stood and said he needed to get back to work. "You boys stay safe."

Ben thanked Officer Silver for his time, and the boys quickly added their thanks as well. "That was a great story," Tyler said.

Once Officer Silver left the diner, Ben began explaining the plan for the rest of the day. "We'll go check in at the hotel to give us some time to relax while I work on a script. Then once it gets dark, we'll shoot in a patch of woods across the street from the fenced in area," Ben told them. "It'll give a nice ominous visual as I explain the legend and give more details about the accidents it has caused."

Sean wiped his face carefully with a paper napkin. "You won't need me for woods duty. I'll stay in the motel and process the video from this afternoon."

"Sounds like a plan," Ben agreed.

"A terrible plan!" Tyler waved his hands around as he spoke. "We'll be in the woods in the dark. Exactly like Officer Silver was when the Goat Man jumped on him."

"That was probably not the Goat Man," Sean said. "It was probably a trespasser."

"I'd rather not take that chance," Tyler grumbled, slumping down in his seat.

"We won't be under the trestle." Ben hauled Tyler up out of the chair. "We'll be fine."

Tyler clumped along behind Ben as they walked to the counter to pay for their food. "Famous last words."

By the time night fell, and they drove out to the woods, Tyler had been sulking and muttering for hours. He'd barely even eaten supper. Since Gabe didn't know what to say to help his friend feel better, he just ignored the grumbling. He knew from experience that once they got into the woods, Tyler would do the job.

At least, that's what Gabe expected. They pulled off the highway onto a narrow dirt road across from the trestle fence. Ben drove along the bumpy road until he saw a spot to pull off. "Grab the night vision camera," he called to Gabe. "And Tyler, you grab the small camera and a light. I don't want to just shoot with night vision. It's not clear enough."

"And we want the audience to clearly see us get jumped on," Tyler grumbled.

Gabe had to give his friend credit. As unhappy as Tyler was, he followed Ben's directions quickly, though not without complaint. Loaded with gear, Gabe and Tyler followed Ben down a narrow path in the woods.

When Tyler stepped on the back of Gabe's shoe for the second time, Gabe whispered, "Could you not follow so close?"

"In horror movies, the guy following too far back gets eaten first," Tyler whispered loudly. "I am not getting eaten!"

"Shh," Gabe said. "Ben is ready."

"Humans have long been afraid of the dark," Ben said, looking over his shoulder at

the camera as he began to recite his script. "In the dark, we can imagine all kinds of monsters. Some might even be real. We are in Kentucky to explore one of the strangest and most dangerous legends we've ever encountered. The Pope Lick Monster, who many call the Goat Man."

Tyler shuddered next to Gabe. Then they all jumped as a piercing scream cut through the darkness. Someone was in trouble!

chapter 8

THE
CHASE

They barely had time to look at one another before a teenaged girl ran down the path and practically climbed into Ben's arms. Gabe kept filming. He knew they'd have to get the girl's permission to use the video, but at least they'd have the footage if she agreed.

"I saw the monster!" the teenager gasped into Ben's face. "It's out there!"

Ben gently held her at arm's length. "Are you all right?"

She bobbed her head. "I ran before it could get me." Then she looked around wildly. "We have to get out of the woods!"

"If you want, you can wait in our van. You'll be safe there." Ben turned toward Tyler. "Can you lead this young lady out to the van? Give the camera to Gabe and hand me the light."

"Sure." Tyler handed off the gear then he squared his shoulders and took the girl's arm. "Come on. It's going to be fine."

Even though she was a lot taller than Tyler, she just nodded and followed him meekly down the path. Gabe was proud of his friend. He knew Tyler was pretending to be brave to help the girl calm down. As soon as Tyler and the girl had vanished down the trail, Ben waved for Gabe to follow him.

As Ben held up the light to shine on the trail ahead, Gabe watched the viewfinder of the camera. The camera captured the shadowy path with a kind of silvery glow. Gabe strained to listen, trying to hear the sound of anything moving in the woods. All he heard was the high-pitched whine and chirp of night insects.

Ben pushed a branch aside, revealing a

small clearing ahead. Gabe gasped as the light shone on a bent figure with tall curling horns. The creature looked in their direction only for a moment before darting down the trail.

For a moment Ben and Gabe were so shocked that they stood frozen, staring into the now empty clearing. Then Ben shook off his surprise and called, "Come on. We can't let it get away."

With Ben's longer legs, it was all Gabe could do to keep up as his big brother stormed down the trail. The light Ben held swung wildly as he ran, and gave Gabe only brief glimpses through the dark woods. Sometimes Gabe thought he saw strange flashes of light, almost like low flying fireflies, but he suspected it was just Ben's light reflecting back at them from things in the woods.

Finally, they reached another clearing. Ben stopped and flashed his light around. And there, in the middle of a bramble thicket, they spotted the Goat Man staring out at them.

"Over here." Ben stormed through the clearing and shoved aside the thorny canes with the light in his hand. He thrust his arm into the brush and pulled out the Goat Man's head.

Gabe yelped as Ben held up the head by one of the horns. Then Gabe realized he was looking at a thin, floppy skin with empty eyes. "I think we found Chester's mask," Ben said. "I think we know who was wearing this."

Gabe frowned. "Who?"

"Chester's friend Jake." He gave Gabe a knowing smile. "Like you, I noticed his bulging bag seemed about the right size for a costume."

"You didn't say anything," Gabe said.

"I didn't have any proof. We still don't. But maybe Chester will figure it out once he gets the mask back."

They poked around in the woods for a bit longer, but saw no sign of anyone in a Goat Man costume. Ben and Gabe finally headed back to the van. Ben pulled open the door to reveal Tyler playing cards with the teenaged girl.

She shrieked when she saw the Goat Man head in Ben's hand. "It's okay," Ben said, holding the head up. "It's just a mask. Someone played a trick on you."

The girl glared at the mask. "Well, that's just mean! That thing scared me half to death."

"Why were you in the woods?" Ben asked.

She blushed slightly and pulled a phone out of her hoodie pocket. "I was filming a video about the Goat Man. I didn't expect to actually see it!" Then she frowned again. "Though I guess I didn't really."

"It looked real," Gabe said. "And scary."

Ben offered to take the girl home, and she readily agreed. She didn't live far away and as soon as she hopped out of the van, Ben pulled out his phone. "I'm going to call Chester and see if he wants his head back."

It turned out that he did and the team drove through the dark to Chester's house. "You know what I think," Tyler sang out from a seat in the back of the van. "I think the Goat Man is Officer Silver. He likes scaring people. I bet he does it to keep anyone from wanting to meet the Goat Man."

"That's an interesting theory," Ben said. "But I'm pretty sure it's wrong."

"No, hold on. Don't shut me down yet," Tyler added. "He patrols that area. He'd know it really well. That's probably why he got away when you chased him."

"Maybe," Ben agreed, though he didn't

sound like he really thought Tyler's theory was possible.

Gabe held the mask in his lap as he rode in the front passenger seat. He thought about the hunched figure of the Goat Man and the strange flashes of light. He was fairly sure Ben was right about one thing. Officer Silver wasn't the Goat Man. But he thought he knew who was!

chapter 9

AN UNUSUAL MONSTER

Chester Freed stood on the porch as they pulled up in front of his house. As soon as Gabe hopped out of the van with the Goat Man's head, Chester called out, "That's my mask all right. Thanks for bringing it back to me."

"Someone used it to scare a teenager," Ben said. "Would any of your friends do something like that?"

Chester winced. "Maybe." He held open the door. "You guys want to come in?"

They walked into the living room of the house. "You know it wasn't me, right?" Chester asked. "I mean, I like publicity for the attraction, but not this time of year."

"I believe you," Ben said. "But I think we

ought to consider your friend Jake. He had that tote bag that was full of something."

Chester rubbed the side of his nose. "Jake said that was laundry."

"Laundry you hadn't noticed him carrying," Ben reminded him.

"I don't know. I can be absentminded," Chester said. "I really don't think Jake would take the suit without asking. He knows I'd loan it to him if he wanted it. Why not just ask?"

Tyler spoke up then. "Maybe because he was going to use it for a prank you might not approve of?"

Chester kept shaking his head. "No. Jake would have just asked."

"Actually," Gabe said. "I think you're right."

Everyone turned to look at him in surprise. Before Gabe could answer, Chester's mom walked in with a tray of cookies. "I thought I heard you boys in here," she sang out.

"They found my Goat Man mask," Chester said. "And Ben here says he thinks maybe Jake took it."

"Oh, I don't know about that," she said brightly. "Wouldn't Jake simply ask you to borrow it?"

"That's what I said!"

His mother patted his cheek. "You're so clever. You and your friends too." She beamed at all of them.

Gabe smiled back at her. "Not as clever as you, ma'am. You made a great Goat Man tonight. We totally believed it."

"What?" Chester said. "Mom wasn't out in the woods playing Goat Man tonight."

"Actually, I was," she said. Then she beamed at Gabe. "Did you think I was scary?"

"Terrifying," Gabe assured her.

"See," she said, looking at her son. "I told you that you should let me be in your attraction. I can be scary! You ask these young men. This is a family business, you should let me be part of it."

Chester blinked at his mom. "You were the Goat Man?"

She nodded proudly. "And I scared these tough young men silly. I also scared that poor girl." She sighed and looked up at Ben. "Did you get her name? I should send her some cookies as an apology."

"She'd probably like that," Ben agreed.

Chester sighed deeply. "Well, I guess you proved your point. You can be our monster this year."

Ben and the boys left soon after. Judging by his bulging pockets, Gabe suspected Tyler had some extra cookies to take back to the motel. Gabe figured Tyler deserved them.

"You did a great job of calming that girl down," he whispered to Tyler as they walked to the van.

"I was just glad I wasn't the one chasing the Goat Man." He leaned closer to Gabe. "Was that little old lady really scary?"

"Yeah, she really was."

Ben pulled open the van door. "Let's go pick up Sean and go out for pie. That diner we ate lunch at had a great pie menu."

Gabe and Sean quickly agreed as they hopped into the van.

When they got back to the motel room, Ben followed Tyler and Gabe into the room. They found Sean with his nose almost pressed to the screen of his laptop. Tyler grabbed Sean by the wrist. "Work later," he sang out. "Pie now!"

Sean pulled his arm loose and pointed toward the screen. "Hold on. There's something Ben needs to see here."

"What?" Ben asked.

As Sean cued up some of the video of Ben talking to the camera about the Goat Man, Sean said, "Just watch." He pressed a key and the video began to play. They saw Ben's serious face as he talked about the dangerous rail trestle that hung far above them. The trestle itself wasn't on the video, just one of the rust-spotted supports.

Gabe figured they'd captured a glimpse of Officer Silver through the brush. He kept his eye on the shrubs behind the chain-link fence. He expected to see something move. Nothing did. Sean stopped the video and turned to look at them. "Did you see it?"

"I only saw me," Ben said.

"I was watching the brush," Gabe said. "Nothing moved."

"Yeah, are you pranking us?" Tyler asked.

"Look again, but don't watch the bushes, watch the trestle support."

This time Gabe kept his attention on the trestle as his brother talked. At first, he didn't see anything, then he must have shifted the camera slightly because he could see an edge of the trestle support that hadn't shown before. Something was clinging to the metal. Something with a huge head, or maybe a head with huge horns. Sean froze the image on the screen.

"Do you think that's the thing that jumped on Officer Silver?" Tyler whispered.

"I do not know the answer to that," Sean said. "It maybe just be an illusion caused by light and shadow."

"Do you think it is?" Gabe asked.

"No," Sean told him, turning around. "I think it's the Goat Man."

Gabe stared at the shadowy shape on the side of the trestle support. They'd probably never know if they'd gotten a video of the Pope Lick Monster, but he looked up at his friends with a grin. "Whatever it is," he said. "It's so cool."

And that, they could all agree with.